Little Cloud by Eric Carle

Scholastic Inc.
New York   Toronto   London   Auckland   Sydney

The clouds drifted slowly across the sky.
Little Cloud trailed behind.

The clouds pushed upward and away.
Little Cloud pushed downward and
touched the tops of the houses and trees.

The clouds moved out of sight.
Little Cloud changed into a giant cloud.

Little Cloud changed into a sheep.
Sheep and clouds sometimes look alike.

Little Cloud changed into an airplane.
Little Cloud often saw airplanes
flying through the clouds.

Little Cloud changed into a shark.
Little Cloud once saw a shark
through the waves of the ocean.

Little Cloud changed into two trees.
Little Cloud liked the way trees never
moved and stayed in one place.

Little Cloud changed into a rabbit.
Little Cloud loved to watch rabbits
dash across the meadows.

Then Little Cloud changed into a hat. Because . . .

Little Cloud changed into a clown and needed a hat.

The other clouds drifted back.
They huddled close together.
"Little Cloud, Little Cloud," they called. "Come back."
Little Cloud drifted toward the clouds.

Then all the clouds changed into one big cloud and

rained!